MEET THE LIBRARIAN/
CONOCE A LOS BIBLIOTECARIOS

By Joyce Jeffries   Traducción al español: Eduardo Alamán

Gareth Stevens
Publishing

Please visit our website, www.garethstevens.com. For a free color catalog of all our high-quality books, call toll free 1-800-542-2595 or fax 1-877-542-2596.

Library of Congress Cataloging-in-Publication Data

Jeffries, Joyce.
Meet the librarian = Conoce a los bibliotecarios / by Joyce Jeffries.
  p. cm. — (People around town = Gente de mi ciudad)
Parallel title: Conoce a los bibliotecarios.
In English and Spanish.
Includes index.
ISBN 978-1-4339-9468-5 (library binding)
1. Librarians—Juvenile literature. 2. Libraries—Juvenile literature. 3. Occupations—Juvenile literature. I. Jeffries, Joyce. II. Title.
Z665.5 J44 2013
371.425—dc23

First Edition

Published in 2014 by
Gareth Stevens Publishing
111 East 14th Street, Suite 349
New York, NY 10003

Copyright © 2014 Gareth Stevens Publishing

Editor: Ryan Nagelhout
Designer: Nicholas Domiano

Photo credits: Cover, p. 1, © iStockphoto.com/kali9; p. 5 ChameleonsEye/Shutterstock.com; p. 7 TonRo Images/ Thinkstock.com; pp. 9, 23 Digital Vision/Thinkstock.com; pp. 11, 15, 17 iStockphoto/Thinkstock.com;; pp. 13, 19 Comstock/Thinkstock.com; p. 21 OJO Images/OJO Images/Getty Images; p. 24 (computer, blocks) iStockphoto/ Thinkstock.com.

Printed in the United States of America

CPSIA compliance information: Batch #CS13GS: For further information contact Gareth Stevens, New York, New York at 1-800-542-2595.

Contents

Contenido

Librarians love to work with books!

¡A los bibliotecarios les encantan los libros!

They work at a library.

Trabajan en las bibliotecas.

Some work in schools.

Algunos trabajan en
las escuelas.

Their name comes
from the Latin word
for book.

El nombre bibliotecario
viene de la palabra
griega "biblion" que
significa libro.

They can find you
many kinds of books.

Los bibliotecarios te
pueden ayudar a
buscar los libros.

13

You can use their computers. They can show you how to use one.

Puedes usar sus computadoras. Los bibliotecarios pueden enseñarte a usarlas.

You take home books.

Puedes llevarte libros
a casa.

Make sure you bring them back! This is called lending.

¡Acuérdate de regresarlos!
A esto se le llama préstamo.

They also lend
you movies!

¡Las bibliotecas
también prestan
películas!

Some even have toys and games!

¡Algunas también tienen juegos y juguetes!

Words to Know/
Palabras que debes saber

computer /
(la) computadora

toys /
(los) juguetes

Index / Índice

24